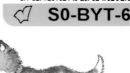

For Reuben – and for his sisters,
Leonie and Emilia

First published in 1998

1 3 5 7 9 10 8 6 4 2

© Text and illustrations Hilda Offen

Hilda Offen has asserted her right under
the Copyright, Designs and Patents Act, 1988,
to be identified as the author and illustrator of this work

First published in the United Kingdom in 1998 by
Hutchinson Children's Books
Random House UK Limited
20 Vauxhall Bridge Road, London SW1V 2SA

Random House Australia (Pty) Limited
20 Alfred Street, Milsons Point, Sydney
New South Wales 2061, Australia

Random House New Zealand Limited
18 Poland Road, Glenfield
Auckland 10, New Zealand

Random House South Africa (Pty) Limited
Endulini, 5A Jubilee Road, Parktown 2193, South Africa

Random House UK Limited Reg. No. 954009

A CIP catalogue record for this book is
available from the British Library

ISBN 0 09 176880 2

Printed in Singapore

MY BLANKET IS BLUE

Sleeptime ⭐ Dreamtime

HILDA OFFEN

HUTCHINSON

London Sydney Auckland Johannesburg

(WHISPER) *My blanket is soft,*
My blanket is blue.

When Mum says, 'Sleep tight',
Do you know what I do?

I say to my friends,
'Are you ready to go?
Let's fly to the North
And play in the snow!'

With the moon to our left
And the stars to our right,
We fly through the sky –
We fly through the night!

My blanket is cuddly –

It's warmer than toast.

I can scare off the bears.
'Shoo, Bears! I'm a ghost!'

(WHISPER) *My blanket is soft,*
My blanket is blue.

'Let's go,' says the cat.
'It's too cold for me!'

So we fly to the South
And swim in the sea.

I can lie in my hammock

Or sit in the shade.

I can play Bouncing Bears
And drink lemonade.

(WHISPER) *My blanket is soft,*
My blanket is blue.

I can stand on my head,

Ask a tiger to tea,

Tuck him up if he's ill.

So – Three Cheers for me!

We can ride on an elephant
Down to the bay

Where my boat will be waiting
To take us away.

We sail on the sea,
We sail through the night –

All the way to my room
Where Mum says, 'Sleep tight!'

My friends sigh and yawn;
They snuggle down, too.

(WHISPER) *My blanket is soft,*
My blanket is blue.